THE · TRUTH · ABOUT
Jack·O·Lanterns

THE · TRUTH · ABOUT

Jack·O·Lanterns

GREEN TIGER PRESS

MMVI

ISBN 1-59583-096-0   ISBN13 978-1-59583-096-8

GREEN TIGER PRESS IS A DIVISION OF LAUGHING ELEPHANT

WWW.LAUGHINGELEPHANT.COM

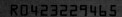

JACK-O'-LANTERNS start as pumpkins, which are grown from seeds.

They create vines that lie on the ground and bear pumpkins which grow big and turn from green to orange.

They are ready to pick just before
Halloween.

Farmers gather them for the market.

And sometimes
people go into the field

To choose their own pumpkins.

Most of us buy them in stores, where they choose pumpkins which they think will look good.

Carving the faces brings them to life

and changes them from
pumpkins
into Jack-O'-Lanterns.

They are **lighted** from the inside,
which will make them the best part
of **Halloween**.

Almost every Jack-O'-Lantern smiles

because they are so glad to be alive.

Their happy smiles are infectious, and everyone around them is soon **smiling**.

They do enjoy scaring people,

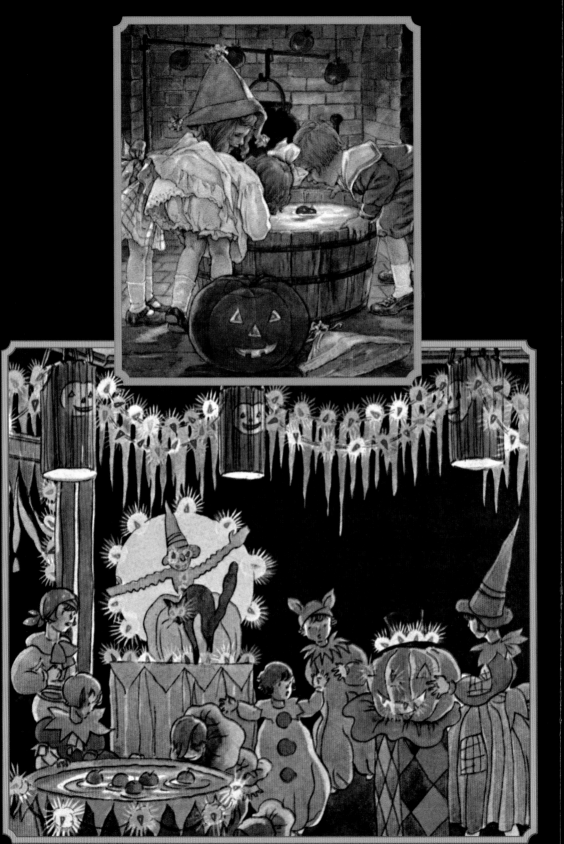

Jack-O'-Lanterns love
to be invited to **parties**,

and join parades and processions
whenever they get the chance.

They like to **dress up,**

and are especially
fond of hats.

Jack-O'-Lanterns enjoy the company of owls and black cats,

and help **witches** in any way they can.

They seldom get the chance
to move about,

but the few who get to
enjoy it thoroughly.

Late on Halloween night,
when all the people have gone to bed
they have parties of their own.

They **frolic** until dawn,
for this has been the best night
of their lives, and they want to enjoy
its every moment.

PICTURE CREDITS